MISFIT

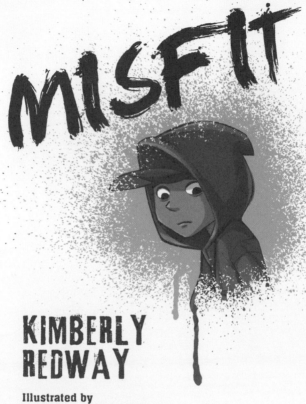

KIMBERLY REDWAY

Illustrated by
ARTFUL DOODLERS

BLOOMSBURY EDUCATION

LONDON   OXFORD   NEW YORK   NEW DELHI   SYDNEY

CONTENTS

Chapter One   7

Chapter Two   21

Chapter Three   32

Chapter Four   41

Chapter Five   51

Chapter Six   59

Chapter Seven   66

Chapter One

"You are a tramp and you come from a family of chavs," Ollie shouted. I could not help myself. I felt the anger rise inside me. We were always scrapping, but my next punch was going to hit home.

It was the fifth time this term that he had said things about my family. I was so angry it nearly choked me. I had already been in a few fights at school, most of them with Ollie Cooper. This time I was going to get the better of him.

All I could feel was my fist clenching. This time he had gone too far. I charged towards him and hit him.

"George Turner!" Mr Thames shouted across the playground. The crowd that was around us parted as he walked up to us.

I stopped and span around. "He called me a tramp, Sir. He said I come from a family of chavs..."

Mr Thames's eyes lacked their usual warmth. "Off to Mr Foster's office, George, and you too, Ollie."

"But, Sir," I began, but Mr Thames was having none of it.

"Now!" he shouted.

We walked in and Ollie barged past me, knocking me with his shoulder. It was so hard I only just stopped myself from falling. We slumped down into chairs just outside Mr Foster's office.

My head was bowed as rage churned in my stomach. I imagined the smirk on Ollie's face. His blue eyes were dazzling now but I had given him a good punch. He would have a black eye soon.

"George Turner," Mr Foster shouted. "In my office now, lad."

I walked in and shut the door behind me.

"So?" Mr Foster said. His face was furious. His green eyes sparked with anger.

"He said my family were chavs, Sir," I exploded. "He's always having a go." Mr Foster's eyebrows dipped low into a frown.

"Sit down, George," he said.

"And Sir…" But before I could continue he held up a large flat hand. "How many times have I had to call you to this office? The answer is countless times. You have been cautioned before. You have learnt nothing."

"But…"

"No, this time you have gone too far. You are permanently excluded from this school."

"But… Sir." All my dreams flashed through my mind. I wanted to get high marks in my GCSEs and then… become a detective – a really cool one like the ones on TV. I needed to stay at Hawthorn Grammar. Mr Foster was shaking his head. I hung my head and shame burnt through me.

* * * * *

I sat in the living room at home while my parents went into school. Three of my brothers were sitting around on the sofas. I had the loser's spot on the floor. While I got stuck into a graphic novel, my brothers watched music videos. On the television there were men in baggy shirts. They were wearing heavy jewellery and they all seemed to have gold teeth. The men's mouths moved quickly as they spat their lyrics.

Kyle was rapping along, even saying the swear words because Dad was not around. I didn't let anyone see me roll my eyes at Kyle. He always behaved like a wannabe rapper. Suddenly Oscar grabbed my book and chucked it to Kyle.

"What are you reading now, coconut?" Oscar asked, cackling.

"Coconut?" I asked stupidly. I knew better than to try to get my book back. They would probably just hold me down and laugh.

"Yeah – because you're brown on the outside," Kyle said, and turned the book over with disgust, "but white in the middle."

My other brothers laughed.

"I'm not a coconut, I'm black. I'm no more a coconut than you are," I said, annoyed.

"Yeah, you're straight up gangsta," Ryan said. That stung because he was usually the nicest of the three.

He turned round to the others, laughing. "Remember when our little coconut thought '50 Cent' was money when everyone knows he's like the most famous rapper ever?"

Ryan is the second eldest of my brothers. He is also the shortest, but all my brothers are huge. I'm lanky and thin compared to them. Ryan is eighteen – he has a lot of facial hair and is always trimming his beard.

"Remember when he thought 'Grime' was what you get under the sink?" said Oscar, joining in. Oscar is fifteen – the youngest of my older brothers and built like a truck. He is always wearing baggy everything – baggy t-shirts, baggy tracksuit bottoms – and it just looks great. If I wear anything baggy I look skinny and ridiculous.

"But I **am** black," I protested. "Being black doesn't mean you have to be a rapper or wear gangster clothes!"

Kyle is sixteen and tough. He wears all these chains around his neck. I always wonder, if rappers started wearing bike chains, would he do the same? "Black people have had it rough for years and years," said Kyle. "After all they've been through, after their **struggle**. Do you want black people to suffer more, by you pretending to fit in? You are no tough guy like us."

"Here," Kyle said chucking the book to me. "Coconut boy. What is that rubbish anyway?"

"It's a graphic novel," I said, realising I sounded stuck-up.

"What, like a kids' comic?" Oscar cackled.

"No, it's a... never mind," I said and sighed. There was no point in trying to explain.

My brothers just sat laughing together as they turned their attention back to the TV.

* * * * *

Then Dad came into the room.

"You'll have to go to Kingsworth School with your brothers," he said. He hadn't even said hello to any of us.

"No, Dad!" I shouted.

"George wouldn't last a day," Oscar said. "No way is he coming to our school."

"Seriously Dad, please don't let him spread his geek germs around our school," Oscar said. He dropped to his knees on the floor, dramatically. "I am **begging** you!"

"What else can we do?" Dad asked. He turned to me and his eyes flashed with anger. "You've completely mucked up your chances, George. I'm very disappointed in you."

Mum shook her head. She had her permed hair cut short and always managed to look stylish. She was dressed in a mustard yellow dress, with horse earrings, and a purple scarf around her neck. Dad had his thick dreadlocks pulled back from his face and held in place by a red elastic band. He was dressed in an African tunic.

"We didn't raise you to fight like an alley cat," Mum said, shaking her head. "Go to your room, George, and think about the future you've just destroyed."

Chapter Two

Surprise, surprise, there was a space for me at Kingsworth School. So the next morning, I was dressed in one of Oscar's old uniforms – the shirt billowed out and the trousers kept making a break for the ground.

At the breakfast table Jethro sat eating a fried plantain sandwich. Jethro is my oldest brother. He went to university but now he works in the Spar down the road.

"Hey George," Jethro said, giving me a nod.

I met his gaze and he grinned.

Triss is my older sister – a "woman of colour", as she calls herself. She is nineteen and wears her hair natural because she doesn't believe in perms, weaves or extensions. Right now her hair was twisted around her head and she wore a black wrap. She sat at the breakfast table eating a melon slice. She always has an opinion on everything. No one likes arguing with Triss.

Triss glared at me as I came into the kitchen. I pretended I hadn't seen and I tucked into a fried English breakfast made by Mum. Mum always cooked when she was stressed. She would wake up early in the morning and put together the whole works. It was too bad I was the cause of the stress but what she'd made was delicious.

"So that's that," Triss snapped at me. "You can't control yourself and now what? You get kicked out of school for fighting."

"Ollie called our family a bunch of chavs," I whined. Even I knew that this wasn't a good enough reason to beat someone up.

"We are going to get off to school," Kyle said, walking in with a black string bag. Oscar was with him. They were dressed properly now but I knew that as they walked out of the house their ties would get looser and their trousers would hang lower.

"Oh no you don't," Mum said, folding her arms. "Wait for George."

I felt a little hurt to see my brothers didn't want to wait for me. They tutted and groaned at Mum.

I finished my breakfast and followed after them. Once we'd reached the front door Oscar pushed his hand against my chest.

"Stay seven steps behind us at all times," he said, gruffly.

They made me count the steps as I stepped backwards. Then they proceeded to talk loudly about me as we walked.

"... And that backpack," Kyle said, laughing. "What an absolute dork! He's going to get thumped at school."

"Yes!" Oscar shouted before giving Kyle a high five. "I mean, the backpack, with those clothes and the whole geeky attitude... ain't that true, brother?"

I knew there was no point asking if they would back me up in a fight. Despite the fact that I had always defended **them** I knew I could not expect the same.

* * * * *

We arrived at Kingsworth School and my
mouth dropped open. Sure, I'd seen it when
I'd gone past on the bus to my old school, but
up close it looked even more run-down. There
was litter all over the grassy area out front,
some of the windows had black tape across
them and it could certainly do with a new
coat of paint.

"Welcome to the palace," Oscar said,
laughing, as we walked in. He must have
forgotten he said he was not going to talk
to me. They walked over to their friends and
fist-bumped, leaving me to find my own
way to the school office.

The secretary gave me a funny look when I told her my name was George Turner.

"You are one of the Turner boys, huh?" she asked, narrowing her eyes.

"Yes, Miss," I said as sweetly as I could manage, and her lips spread into a smile. "The head teacher is in a meeting so Bette, your year's team captain, will show you around the school. She will be your school buddy for the first week."

"Who's Bette...?"

I turned to my right. I had been about to roll my eyes. The last thing I needed was some eager loser sticking to my side the whole time. I was already a target just because of being me. The last thing I needed was some... then I turned round and saw her.

Bette was tall. Her hair was in cornrows at the top and the rest defied gravity like a glorious mane. Her large brown eyes blinked at me and she was gorgeous. Her coffee-coloured skin shone, she looked great in her school uniform – and she was staring right at me.

"That would be me," she said, sizing me up with a glance. Then she grinned. "Normally Tyrone would be your buddy, but he's off sick. He has the flu or... something."

"Thank the flu gods!" I thought. Bette offered me her hand and I shook it eagerly, maybe a little too eagerly but she didn't seem to notice. She handed me my planner and timetable. Her fingers brushed against mine as I took them.

"We're in mostly the same classes so…"
she began, and then she frowned deeply at
something behind me.

"Hey, Bette," I heard. "What are you doing
with coconut boy?"

I knew that voice. As I turned round, I knew
who I would see, but I hoped it wouldn't be
true. It was. I saw Oscar towering above me.

Chapter Three

Oscar pushed me aside. It was as though a rock was pushing a twig. I stumbled as he moved closer to Bette, and that's when I knew. He was leaning up against the wall in a way that would show off the muscles underneath his school shirt. His eyebrows were waggling the way they always did when he met a pretty girl. He had made his voice even lower and deeper than usual. My brother Oscar was keen on Bette.

My heart sank. OK, I know I am nothing to look at. I'm just the geeky, lanky kid, so I seriously doubt someone as stunning as Bette would look my way. For a moment I had thought there just might be a chance. But there was no way I could compete with Oscar.

Bette was still frowning. Her arms were folded against her chest and her foot was tapping. She rolled her eyes and breathed through her mouth. I was no body language expert but something told me that she... wasn't interested.

"I'll be your bad boy if you'll be my honey," Oscar said. "Baby I can make you feel so good."

I swallowed a laugh.

"I'm not your baby, Oscar," Bette snarled. "So if you'd just let me get on with…"

She tried to walk around him but he grabbed at her arm and pulled her back towards him. He leaned down and looked into her gorgeous eyes. Something came over me. He shouldn't be allowed to do this to Bette. The secretary was not looking at us.

"Leave her alone," I shouted.

"What did you say to me?" Oscar said as he dropped Bette's arm.

"Nothing... I mean..." I began. Bette poked a finger in his chest before I could carry on.

"Listen, bog breath," she said, "I'm not interested in you. Take a hint. Come on George."

She slipped an arm through mine and before Oscar could pound me into the ground we walked away. I felt a little light-headed – I had gone up against Oscar and I was still alive. I looked at my arms and legs just to check – yep, still attached.

"I just hate guys like that," Bette was saying as we walked through the school hall and then suddenly I realised I was the centre of attention. Other boys were staring at me and looking at Bette like she was a goddess.

"They think they are so macho but really they are idiotic. You know what I mean?" asked Bette.

"So... um, what kind of guys do you like?" I asked, bravely.

"Well, that would be telling," she said and grinned.

I grinned back – life was not so bad.

Bette stopped walking and stared into my eyes, and there it was: a tingling inside me. "Thank you for what you said back there," Bette said.

"It's no big deal," I said shrugging. She was still looking at me in that way.

She put a hand over mine. "No, I'm serious. Thank you."

We walked along the corridor.

"Oscar is such a show-off ," Bette said. "Do you know him?"

"Um... he's my brother," I said, heart hammering. Would that change how she saw me?

She laughed.

"Wow, you don't look alike."

I had heard it all before. Oscar was bigger than me, taller than me and fitter than me.

"Here we are," she said once we got to a room called 408. There was a line of kids outside the door. Everyone looked bored and was either leaning against the wall or inspecting their nails. A male teacher walked out of the room and began yelling.

"You will stand in this line until you're ready to enter the classroom like civilised individuals. If you all stomp inside like a pack of wild animals we will line up again."

He turned and marched back inside the classroom.

"Your first class is science," Bette said, pointing at the timetable I held in my hand. "Mine is maths, so I'll meet you outside this room after the bell has gone."

"G-g-great," I said and I grinned at her.

"See you then," she said waggling her fingers before walking off. I stood in the middle of the hallway watching her leave.

Then I felt a hard shove from behind me.
I stumbled over my own feet and landed in
a heap on the floor. I sat up and looked
up at my attacker. Of course it was Oscar.
He grinned.

Chapter Four

Peals of laughter filled the hall and seemed to bounce off the walls. I scrambled to my feet and glared at Oscar, but was careful not to make him too angry. It was no good – an insect standing up to a lion had more of a chance.

Oscar obviously liked everyone laughing and he turned and grinned round at all the kids in the hall. He just wanted to make me look stupid. I didn't have to look around to know that everyone was waiting to see what would happen next.

"Well, that's the price you need to pay for breathing the same air as me," he said, and turned away.

"You're just jealous," I said, thinking of Bette. That was a big mistake. Oscar turned around almost as if in slow motion. Then he charged over to me. I flinched and he laughed. I noticed that even the teacher was watching the show with his arms folded.

"Listen, you are nothing but a snob," Oscar said. "You think you are better than me. Just because you went to that posh school. Well, here you do not have your posh mates. By the time I'm done with you, everyone will know what you are."

He walked away up the corridor. He really was built like the Hulk and he had the manners to match. He turned back and shouted at my new class.

"George here used to go to Hawthorn Grammar," he shouted. "You get me?"

He pounded his fist against his hand and then turned and left.

I looked around. The kids' curiosity had turned to mistrust, and anger had spread through the group. The teacher was over to me in a few strides.

"What's your name?" he asked, suddenly wary.

"George," I said, still thinking about what Oscar had said. I knew he would try and get me after school.

"I've got my eye on you," said the teacher, and then he spoke to the class. "Right, everyone back inside and turn to page fifty-three."

I followed everyone through the door. Then I felt a shove. I turned around, but the boy who'd shoved me just strode past me into the classroom. Everyone took their seats and I waited to have an idea of the seating plan.

"George, I am Mr Williams. Now sit right at the front," the teacher said. "Your brothers' reputations are well known in this school."

"Brothers?" a girl asked, with her head tilted to the side.

"The Turner boys," Mr Williams said, as a ripple of shock moved across the class. "So you just sit there."

For the rest of the lesson, every time I turned around, someone was staring at me. I couldn't tell if it was because I used to go to Hawthorn Grammar or because my second name was Turner. At the end of class, I walked out of the room and bumped into Bette.

"Sorry," I said, rubbing the back of my neck.

She blinked at me.

"Right, you're doing PE next," she said. "I'll show you where the changing rooms are."

"And you... what are you doing now?" I asked. I groaned to myself. Why was I so awkward?

"PE," she said, smiling. "Come on... grammar boy."

"You know about that?" I asked as we began to walk.

"Uh-huh," she said. "I'm usually the first with gossip. You should have told me."

Was she teasing me? No, that would have been too good to be true.

"Here we are," she said. "See you later... posh lad."

The stench of the small changing rooms hit me before I even entered.

She grinned and walked off. I changed in silence, thinking about the dimples that appeared on her cheeks when she smiled, the tilt of her head when she talked and the shine in her eyes when she spoke.

As I charged out onto the football field, a foot shot out and I sprawled on the grass. A boy held a hand out to pull me up. It was the same boy who had shoved me in class. I took his hand warily and then he let me drop back into the mud. Laughter followed me as I got to my feet.

This wasn't the end of my troubles. When I got back to the changing rooms I found my exercise books had been shredded.

"Did you do this?" I asked one of the boys, who was grinning. He was Asian with thick shaggy hair and spots.

"What if I did?" he asked, laughing. "He's not like his brothers, is he?" he said turning to the others.

"No, he is not," another lad said. His hair was gelled into a quiff.

"We can do whatever we like," he said. "It's like payback for everything they've ever done."

I sucked down the urge to clock him one and suddenly I'd had enough. I shoved my clothes into my bag and walked out of the changing rooms.

Bette was waiting in the corridor.

"George, where are you going?" Bette asked.

I didn't answer her, because even I didn't know.

Chapter Five

I started heading out of school. Fear was gnawing at my insides. I walked through the school grounds and straight out of the gate. I expected to be stopped at any moment, but there was no one to stop me.

I kept my head down, just in case a teacher appeared. I was **done**. I could put up with my brothers picking on me, but I couldn't fight a whole class just because they thought I was a snob and not as tough as my brothers.

I came to a park and went in through the little iron gate. Two of the swings were twisted over the bar at the top and one hung low. I sat on it and looked around at the sorry sight that was a children's playground. The see-saw had graffiti all over it and the slide was closed off.

"Hey, are you OK?" I heard behind me. I whipped around. Bette was standing there, twisting her fingers. Had she followed me? She must have done unless she was a mind-reader.

I just sat there watching her as the wind played with her skirt.

"Are you trying to talk to me in my mind like Professor X?" she asked. "Or are you just not going to answer?"

She was smiling uncomfortably. How could this girl be even slightly interested in me, enough to follow me? I wanted so much to just get up and walk over to her. I wanted to flirt with her and have those big eyes stare into mine. My mind was whispering, "forget Oscar, ask her out. Forget everything, ask her out."

"So are you using telepathy?" she asked.

"I..." I said and then looked down at the ground.

"So he does speak?" she said, venturing forward. "So... we should go back to school."

"You go," I said. "I'm fine, staying right here."

"Oh, OK," she said. "I'd better go back."

She searched my face, for what I wasn't sure.

"The other kids... there's always this battle between our school and Hawthorn Grammar..." she began.

"I know," I said.

"But if anyone's saying things just tell the head of year, he'll sort it," she said.

There it was. She didn't think I was tough enough to defend myself and it had always been that way. When would I be able to stop having to prove myself? Guys came up to me all the time expecting weakness, and I handled it.

I lashed out when no adult was looking and sometimes then they left me alone. I didn't need any teacher's help.

"I can sort it myself," I said.

"Right," she said. "See you."

I watched her walk away, knowing that I'd missed a moment and all because I wasn't like my brothers. They would have just thrown an arm around her, pulled her close and whispered in her ear... well, I never knew what kind of things they said. All I did know was I was so sick of being me. I jumped up and began making my way home.

All the time I walked my mind was whirring. It was like a Google search throwing up answers. "Be more bold," it was saying.

"Have more courage. Be more like Kyle." That was the answer. Bette didn't seem to fancy Oscar, but she would probably go for Kyle. I just had to study him and I'd be like him.

I needed inspiration, so I walked straight into Kyle's smelly room where musty-smelling socks were drying on his radiator. Without Mum's interference, I doubt he would wash anything at all. There was one book in the whole room and I recognised it as my missing Harry Potter. I'd looked everywhere for that.

Kyle's clothes were piled high on the floor. His walls were covered in posters of beautiful women. I picked up his MP3 player and listened to the playlist he'd got cued up. While the music played I looked around.

What I was looking for, I wasn't sure. I just needed to get more of an idea of my brother. First there were his clothes, baggy trousers. So I needed some of them. Next, I could spit lyrics like him – I'd freestyle and attract Bette that way. I just needed to copy him.

Suddenly, I was pushed from behind for the second time that day. I pulled the earphones out of my ears and faced Kyle.

"What are you doing in my room?" he shouted. Kyle looked really angry.

Chapter Six

"Looking for my book," I said, with my heart thumping, and I turned and faced my huge, angry brother. I picked up the Harry Potter and tried to edge out of his room.

"And you are listening to my music because...?" he asked, fiercely snatching the earphones out of my ears.

"You have such great taste," I said. "I just wanted to..."

I paused because honestly I had no idea how to explain myself, but Kyle was nodding.

"Of course you're sick of all that posh white-boy music," he said, nudging me out of his room. "You need some Dancehall in your life."

"Wait, what are **you** doing here?" I asked, distracting him from educating me on "good" music.

"Go down into the living room and see for yourself," he said, looking pleased with himself. I crept down the stairs, almost expecting Mum to come back at any moment. I went into the living room. Sitting on the large battered sofa was... a girl. Her thick black hair curled over her shoulder and her eyes were surrounded by a fan of eyelashes.

"Where's Kyle?" she asked, looking confused. Staring down at her fixed everything in my mind. This girl was gorgeous. She was no Bette, but now I was certain that all I had to do to get my dream girl was behave like Kyle. Kyle strode into the room, with his trousers baggy and the top of his boxers on display.

"Aimee, meet George," Kyle said. "George, meet the door."

He shoved me out into the hall. I spent the rest of that afternoon practising freestyling, and I took a pair of Ryan's trousers and tried them on with my school shirt. I decided I would wear them tomorrow. I was ready. Bette was about to fall in love with me.

* * * * *

The next day I dressed in my baggy trousers, creased my shirt and tied my school tie in a knot. I dressed in some bling – a large silver chain around my neck and one of my mum's clip-on earrings. I sat on the bus rapping along to one of the few rappers I knew.

I was getting into character as I played drum and bass on my mobile. I met Bette at the main door to the school. She hadn't seen me walking up. When she saw me, she raised one eyebrow and looked me up and down.

"You look... are those new trousers?" she asked.

"Just going for a new look," I said.

"Right," she said. "Well, let's go in and..."

"What are you dressed as?" Oscar shouted, laughing. He walked in alongside Kyle who was grinning madly.

"You're an embarrassment, kid," Kyle said, cackling.

"Me and my girl are just," I began, but Bette was shaking her head.

"I am not your girl. I don't belong to anyone," she said.

People were beginning to stare at me and suddenly I felt totally silly.

"She don't want you and we don't want you," Oscar said.

"Bette, you know you're warm for my form," I said, but she just looked disgusted.

"I thought you were different, but you're just like those other idiots," Bette said. "Goodbye, George."

She walked off, and I could only watch her go. Oscar and Kyle pushed past me and walked into school.

Chapter Seven

I sat in my bedroom looking in the mirror at my new look. Bette had been avoiding me all day, and who could blame her? It had been so embarrassing. There was a knock on the door and Jethro walked in. Jethro was more like me than my other brothers – and he didn't go on at me the way they did.

I told him about what had happened.

"Listen kid, being black isn't about slang and baggy trousers," he said. "It's not even about rap music, it's about knowing who you are and being that person."

"But Kyle and Oscar get all the girls," I said. "I just want to be normal."

"You are normal," he said. "Anyway, it sounds like Bette liked you better before the makeover."

He paused and grinned. "Wait," he said. "Is that Mum's earring?"

I nodded and hung my head. "Bette will never speak to me again," I said, gloomily.

Jethro looked at me with real sympathy. "Apologise and see how it goes."

It wasn't difficult to find Bette the next day. She was standing with her arms folded by the main school doors. I took a deep breath and walked straight up to her.

"Hi Bette," I said. "I'm George, I like Doctor Who, hate rap and want to be a country singer because they sing wicked songs. I am so sorry about yesterday."

Her face was unreadable, so I launched into an epic version of one of my favourite songs.

Her beautiful lips twitched, so I sang another line with my eyes closed, half caught up in emotion and half afraid of rejection. Had I done enough to wipe away the damage done the day before?

Suddenly I felt something soft pressing against my face. I opened my eyes for a second to see Bette. She was kissing my cheek. It felt like magic. Then everything was ruined by a mocking laugh.

"Isn't this cosy?" Oscar said. "You seriously fancy my dorky kid brother when you can have a real man like me?"

"A real man isn't afraid to put himself out there. You're just a boy," said Bette.

I was no longer afraid of what Oscar would think of me. "You always go on about blood. I'm your brother. You should support me no matter what." I told him, standing tall.

Oscar stopped laughing and frowned.

"We may not like the same things, but I like who I am," I said. "And I am done changing myself."

Oscar rolled his eyes.

"Lame," he said, walking away. No punching, no pushing, and it made me feel good. I could balance my worlds. I was black and a nerd. I could be both.

When I turned round, Bette was smiling at me. I held out my hand and we walked into school together.

Bonus Bits!

GUESS WHO?

There are lots of characters in this story. Each piece of information below is from the story and is about one of the characters. Can you match the character to the fact? The answers are at the end of the book.

1 George Turner

2 Mr Foster

3 Ryan

4 Oscar

5 Kyle

6 Mum

7 Dad

8 Jethro

9 Triss

10 Bette

A He wears an African tunic.

B He is always trimming his beard.

C He went to university.

D He is a head teacher.

E She has short permed hair.

F She has hair in cornrows at the top.

G She is 19 years old.

H He wears everything baggy.

I He is the narrator of the story.

J He is 16 years old.

QUIZ TIME!

Can you answer these questions about the story? There are answers at the end (but no peeking)

1. What does George want to be when he grows up?

   a a detective

   b a rapper

   c a solicitor

   d a singer

2. What is the name of the school George was excluded from?

   a Kingsworth School

   b Queensworth School

   c Ivy Grammar

   d Hawthorn Grammar

3. Which names belong to three of George's brothers?

   a Oscar, Kyle, William

   b Kyle, William, Ollie

   c Oscar, Kyle, Ryan

   d Ryan, Oscar, Ollie

4. What was Kyle singing because Dad wasn't there?

   a unkind words

   b classical songs

   c funny words

   d swear words

5. What is the name of George's new school?

   a Kingsworth School

   b Queensworth School

   c Ivy Grammar

   d Hawthorn Grammar

6. How far behind did George have to walk from his brothers?

    a 7 steps

    b 10 steps

    c 5 steps

    d 3 steps

7. Who was meant to show George on the first day?

    a Bette

    b Tyrone

    c Oscar

    d Ollie

ISSUES

This book deals with some difficult issues. They are, sadly, quite common worries for young people: fitting in, standing up to bullies, trying to be your best and dealing with anger.

Growing up and facing these issues it is important to talk about your feelings and worries with someone.

Childline

Childline is a free, 24-hour counselling service for everyone under 18. Childline says, "You can talk to us about anything. No problem is too big or too small. We're on the phone and online. However you choose to contact us, you're in control. It's free, confidential and you don't have to give your name if you don't want to."

www.childline.org.uk / telephone: 0800 1111

WHAT NEXT?

Have a think about these questions after reading this story:

- Why is it always important to "be true to yourself" and not change because you think others want you to?

- What should you do if you are being bullied by someone?

ANSWERS TO GUESS WHO?

1i, 2d, 3b, 4h, 5j, 6e, 7a, 8c, 9g, 10f

ANSWERS TO QUIZ TIME!

1a, 2d, 3c, 4d, 5a, 6a, 7b